Edgar Badger's Fix-it Day

Edgar Badger's Fix-it Day

by Monica Kulling

illustrated by Neecy Twinem

For Nancy—M.K.

To my Aunt Ellen Thompson,
for her love and encouragement—N.T.

Text copyright © 1997 by Monica Kulling
Illustrations copyright © 1997 by Neecy Twinem

For information contact:
MONDO Publishing
980 Avenue of the Americas
New York, NY 10018
Visit our web site at http://www.mondopub.com

Designed by Eliza Green

Printed in China
05 06 07 08 09   9 8 7 6 5 4 3 2

Library of Congress Cataloging-in-Publication Data
Kulling, Monica.
    Edgar Badger's fix-it day / by Monica Kulling ; illustrated by Neecy
Twinem.
        p.   cm.
    Summary: Edgar Badger finds a way to keep his neighbors happy
even though they complain about the ever-growing pile of junk in his back-
yard.
    ISBN 1-57255-474-6 (pbk. : alk. paper)
    [1.Neighborliness—Fiction. 2. Badgers—Fiction.] I. Twinem, Neecy, ill.
II. Title.
PZ7.K9490155Ed   1997
[E]—dc21   96-38006
                                                                  CIPo
                                                                  AC

Contents

Duncan at the Door

Edgar Badger loved to fix things.
And because he fixed things, he
saved things.

Edgar saved tired tires and sad sofas. He saved bits of string and metal and wood. He saved everything and dumped it all in his backyard. The pile was getting bigger every day.

One morning Edgar woke up to loud
banging on his door. He waddled over
to open it.

There stood his neighbor Duncan
Bear. Duncan had a frown on his
furry face.

"It's happened," said Duncan.

"It has?" replied Edgar. He had no idea what Duncan was talking about.

"I missed the sunrise," said Duncan.

"Really?" replied Edgar.

"You want to know why?" asked Duncan. "I'll tell you why. I missed it because of all the junk in your backyard. That pile is getting so big it's blocking out the sun!"

Duncan sure is gruff this morning, thought Edgar.

"Wait here," Edgar said out loud.

Edgar went inside and came back
with a toaster. Duncan had thrown
it away last week.

"Now your toaster toasts bread and
butters it too!" said Edgar. "Mornings
were made for a bit of buttery toast."

Edgar closed his door. Duncan just stood there admiring his toaster.

A Visit From Violet

Later that morning Edgar was
rooting around in his backyard.
He was looking for wire and wood
to fix a broken window.

Violet Porcupine quietly walked up behind Edgar.

"This yard is an eyesore!" Violet shouted. "Nothing but an eyesore."

Edgar jumped up. Another visiting neighbor. That was two in one day!

But Violet was mad. Her quills bristled with rage. She looked like she might shoot one or two right at Edgar. "Yesterday I was nearly smacked by a runaway tire," said Violet. "It came from your backyard. It was going full speed when it got to my house. I ran out of the way just in time!"

How prickly Violet can be, thought Edgar.

"Wait here," Edgar said out loud. He quickly waddled inside.

Edgar came back with a hard hat. The hat had a telescope on top. He handed the hat to Violet.

"Never let runaway tires push you around," Edgar said. "Get your mind off the everyday. Look to the stars."

Edgar went back to his rooting.

Violet put on her new hat. She peeked
through the telescope. The tiny bird
across the road looked as close as her
front paw.

Worn-out Henry

After lunch Edgar started off for town. He needed to buy nails and paint.

The sun was beating down. But Edgar was cool. He was wearing his sun hat. He had made the hat for sunny days. It had a shade umbrella on top.

On the road Edgar met his neighbor Henry Raccoon. There were dark circles under his eyes.

"I haven't slept a wink in weeks,"
moaned Henry. "I worry about that
junk pile of yours. I ask myself, how
big will it get? . . . what is it all for?"

The sun was high in the sky. Edgar
squinted at Henry.

Henry sure does look worn out,
thought Edgar.

"You need this more than I do," Edgar said out loud.

Edgar took off his hat. He plunked it on Henry's head.

"Here's some shade," Edgar said.

"Now take a nap."

Edgar walked on. Henry lay down for
a nap in the shade.

Sally Speaks Up

Edgar was on his way home. He was loaded down with stuff. He had nails. He had paint. He also had a three-legged table and a two-rung ladder.

Edgar walked up to his house. Sally Otter was sitting on the back porch swing. What a day for visitors!

"I know, I know," said Edgar before Sally even opened her mouth. "You're sick of my junk."

"Well . . . " replied Sally. "That is . . .
your junk is . . . I can't believe . . .
when are you . . ."

Sally sure is acting slippery today,
thought Edgar.

"You ought to get to the point," Edgar
said out loud.

"Your junk is just a mountain of a mess!" shouted Sally. "It's . . . it's . . . mind boggling! What kind of neighbor are you anyway?"

Edgar was surprised. Sally was shy.
She hardly ever said more than
two words in a row. And she *never*
shouted.

Suddenly there was a rustling in the
bushes.

Happy Neighbors

Out popped Duncan from behind the
bushes. Out popped Violet. Out popped
Henry.

"He's our kind of neighbor," they all shouted. "And he's a good neighbor, too!"

"Look at my hat!" cried Henry. "Now I can take naps in the shade." He danced a happy little jig.

"And look at my hat," said Violet. "I can see the tiny birds. I can see the stars at night. And the moon looks as big as a giant balloon!"

"And just look at my toaster," added Duncan. "It toasts bread. It butters bread. And just think, I threw it out."

Sally looked at the wonderful things
Edgar had made. *Edgar does have a
way with junk*, she thought.

Edgar waddled inside and came back
with an amazing inner tube. It had
a basket for food. It had a cooler
for drinks. It had a cushion and an
umbrella. It even had a hook for
holding a book.

Edgar gave the tube to Sally. "Here,"
he said. "Try this on the river."

"Why, it's wonderful," said Sally.
"It's just like home. You *are* a good
neighbor, Edgar."

From that day on, Edgar's neighbors were happy. But Edgar was the happiest one of all. He never stopped fixing things and he never stopped saving things. And he never stopped adding to the pile of junk in his backyard. He just tried to keep it tidy . . .

. . . because happy neighbors are the best neighbors.